This book belongs to:

TAILS FROM THE PANTRY

• Little Life Lessons from Mom and Dad •

Stinky

By Patsy Clairmont

Illustrated by Joni Oeltjenbruns

A Division of Thomas Nelson Publishers
Since 1798

www.thomasnelson.com

TAILS FROM THE PANTRY: STINKY
Text © 2006 by Patsy Clairmont
Illustrations © 2006 by Tommy Nelson®, a Division of Thomas Nelson, Inc.
All rights reserved. No portion of this book may be reproduced in any form
without the written permission of the publisher, with the exception of brief
excerpts in reviews.
Published in Nashville, Tennessee, by Tommy Nelson®, a Division of Thomas
Nelson, Inc.
Tommy Nelson® books may be purchased in bulk for educational, business,
fundraising, or sales promotional use. For information, please e-mail
SpecialMarkets@ThomasNelson.com.

Library of Congress Cataloging-in-Publication Data

Clairmont, Patsy.
  Stinky / by Patsy Clairmont ; illustrated by Joni Oeltjenbruns.
     p. cm. — (Tails from the pantry)
  Summary: Stinky, a mouse who lives in the pantry with his family, recalls the
first time he met his ant friends, Tid and Bit, and their talk about the impor-
tance of being nice.
  ISBN 1-4003-0803-8 (hardcover)
  [1. Kindness—Fiction. 2. Friendship—Fiction. 3. Ants—Fiction. 4. Mice—Fiction.]
I. Oeltjenbruns, Joni, ill. II. Title.
  PZ7.C5276Sti 2006
  [E]—dc22
                                    2005029503

Printed in the United States of America

06 07 08 09 10 WOR 9 8 7 6 5 4 3 2 1

This little series is dedicated to Justin and Noah. . . .

How blessed I am to have two "little mouse" grandsons who regularly nibble in my pantry. Darlings, leave all the crumbs you want in Nana's house. I'll tidy up later. Always heed Mommy and Daddy's lessons about staying safe. You are both loved "a bushel and a peck and a hug around the neck."

~Nana

Once upon a can of sardines sat a mouse named Stinky. Yes, Stinky. His real name, Stephanopolous, seemed to be a lot of letters for a tiny mouse to tote around. And because Stephanopolous loved to gnaw on garlic cloves and nibble onions, he was nicknamed Stinky. He was actually quite proud of his nickname. Stinky thought his name fragrant.

Stinky's mom, Lily, told Stinky that his dad, Mac, almost named him after his favorite hat—fedora. Stinky didn't think *fedora* fit him. Luckily, Mac decided to name his son after his favorite brother, Stephanopolous Metropolis. Stinky lived in the pantry in a forgotten box of Christmas candy with his family.

One morning Stinky was sitting atop the sardine can, awaiting his friends Tid and Bit. Tid and Bit, ants from the baseboard colony, loved to ride in Stinky's vest pocket. It was better than a roller coaster when Stinky jumped from can to can in the pantry.

Up, up

they'd go . . . then

down,
down

they'd come until they reached their favorite spot that they visited every week. Tid and Bit would scurry out of their friend's pocket and head right for the sugar granules at the base of the canister, while Stinky made his way to the bag of garlic cloves for a nibble.

But their friendship hadn't always been such a fun ride. When Tid and Bit first met Stinky, he was mindlessly slurping on an onion. After one especially large slurp, something suddenly stung Stinky's foot. "Ouch!" he cried.

Stinky looked down. There was a broom straw sticking out of his big toe, and beside his foot was Bit yelling up at him, "Don't swallow! You lapped up my brother! He's on your tongue!"

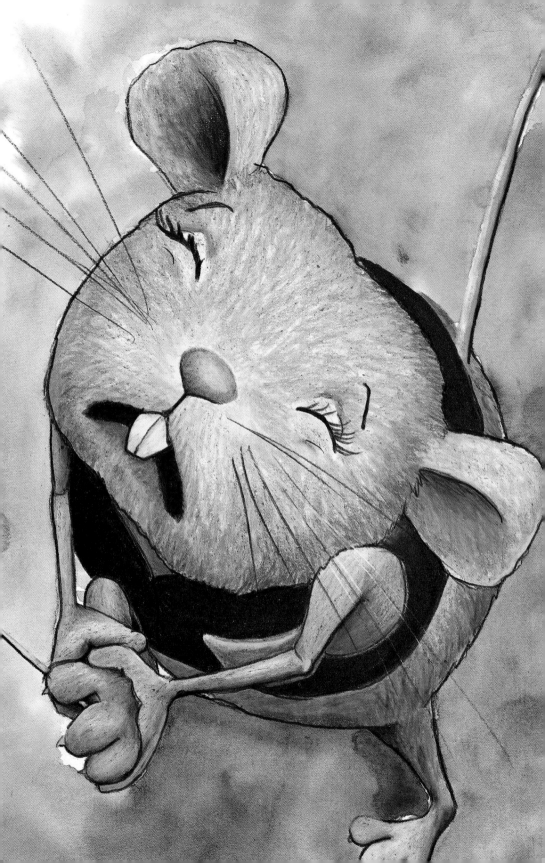

Puzzled, Stinky stuck out his tongue, and sure enough, there was Tid holding on for dear life.

"Sol-ly," Stinky said with his tongue still hanging out. His eyes crossed as he tried to see little Tid. Stinky leaned down to let Tid slide off his tongue. Wet and weak-kneed, Tid was disgusted.

"Sorry," Stinky repeated, "I didn't see you."

"Didn't you ever hear 'look before you lick'?" Tid questioned as he dried himself off.

"No," admitted Stinky. "But I've heard 'look before you *leap*.' My dad has told me that a bunch of times."

"Ants don't leap," Bit stated briskly.

"Are . . . are you guys mad at me?" Stinky asked.

"Well, you almost ate me," Tid pointed out.

"But I said I was sorry," Stinky answered quietly, a tear in his eye.

"Excuse us for a moment,"
Tid said as he and Bit stepped
behind the onion bag to talk it over.

A few minutes later, Bit called up to
Stinky, "Sometimes you just need to give
people time to get over being scared and
angry." Bit paused and then added, "We
forgive you, but please be more careful. You're
not the only animal on the planet, you know."

"Are you guys animals?"

"Well, no. We're insects. But you have to be nice to everyone. Our mom said so."

"Everyone?" Stinky asked. "Even cats?"

"I'm pretty sure cats are on the Be-Nice list," Bit said, scratching his head.

Then Stinky questioned, "What about anteaters? Should we be nice to them?"

"Ooh, nooo, not them," Tid and Bit rang out at the same time.

"But *they're* animals," Stinky insisted.

"Yes, but they eat ants, silly mouse!"

"Well, cats eat mice, silly ants," Stinky said. "And if you haven't noticed, I'm a mice."

"Oh, dear," said Bit as he looked at Tid.

"Maybe we have to be nice to some folks from a distance," offered Tid.

"Maybe," said Bit, thinking. "But, how do we know who to be nice to?" asked Bit, now puzzled.

"I think you can tell by how someone looks if you should be nice," suggested Tid.

"I don't think so," said Stinky, "because Duff is a good-looking calico cat, but he'd eat me for lunch! And you can't tell how nice someone is by a present they offer you 'cause one time Duff left a piece of my favorite cheese on the floor, and when I leaned in to taste it, he tried to swat me with his paw!"

"Oh, Bit, remember when that well-dressed woodpecker told us he'd give us a ride to the top of the tree if we'd step out of our anthill?" Tid asked.

"That's right, Tid. Sooo, how do we know *who* to be nice to?" asked Bit, now even more puzzled than before.

"I think we ask our parents to help us make a Be-Nice list. They're more older and no anteaters or cats have eaten them yet, so they must know," announced Stinky.

"Good idea," agreed Tid and Bit, relieved to have an answer.

"Stinky?"

"Yes, Bit?"

"Did I ever tell you I was sorry for sticking you in the toe with that straw?"

"Nope."

"Well, I'm sorry. I just didn't know how else to get your attention before you swallowed Tid."

"I understand."

"Stinky?"

"Yes, Bit?"

"You're on our Be-Nice list, right at the top."

"Thank you, Tid and Bit, you're on *my* list too!"